MISTS OF TIME

Poems, short stories and extracts

SAM GRANT

© Sam Grant 2018

The rights of Sam Grant to be identified as the author of this work have been asserted by him in accordance with the Copyright, Designs and Patents Act of 1988.

All rights reserved; no part of this publication may be reproduced, stored in a retrieval system, or transmitted in any form or by any means, electronic, mechanical, photocopying, recording or otherwise without the prior written consent of the publisher or a licence permitting copying in the UK issued by the Copyright Licensing Agency Ltd. www.cla.co.uk

ISBN 978-1-78222-620-8

Book design, layout and production management by Into Print
www.intoprint.net
+44 (0)1604 832149

Contents

FOREWORD: 5

PART ONE – POEMS:

    Robyn Hode. 8

    Circle of Life. 11

    Epic Poem: Mists of Time. 14

    Breaking Free, Imagined Interlude. 37

    Eternal Love: An Invitation. 40

    Fun in the Sun – Sea, Pebbles, Sand.. 42

    Light and Darkness. 45

    Free Your Mind: Freedom is a Skateboard 47

    They Gave All.. 49

    Financial Picture Book. 54

    Sleep Departs – Memory Brings Forward the Future 56

    Summer Intruder.. 58

    We Meet-We Part-We Meet 60

    Winter Like Loathe? Not Forever.. 62

    Championship Week. 65

    Limerick: Alpine Love 69

PART TWO – SHORT STORIES:
- Mars Landing with Upgrade for Scott 72
- The Manor House 75
- Atlantic Hijack 89
- Dancing on the Beach 96
- Station Encounter 103
- Secret Cave 113
- Witch Takes Over Village. 135

Foreword

"Mists of Time," the poem, within this publication, was originally in response to compose an epic poem for a competition. A condensed journey. There is the leafy lane metaphor with events at a farm in summer, through to an early sea career into later life.

A remainder of Poems selected, were composed from 2016 through to 2018. At time of writing several have been chosen, and scheduled for 2018 publication in anthologies and books. Others have been composed whilst a novel or novels have been progressing into draft form. A stand-alone short story has preceded development before a novel.

An extract chapter from "Atlantic Hijack," Dancing on the Beach," by Sam Grant and Galactic Mission have been included. Each of these chapters evolved from an original short story format. "Atlantic Hijack," action mystery novel first published in 2014 was conceived as an idea with early chapters first written in 1985 with the working title of "Pilot's Daughter."

Secret Cave is a short story with detailed depiction of sail boat sailing. A reflection from the author's young life, before the author embarked on a career in the Merchant Service.

Please check out these other publications by Sam Grant author of Mists of Time.

Atlantic Hijack (978-1-78222-291-0) Action, mystery novel set in the nineteen-sixties.

River Escape (978-1-78222-574-4) sequel to Atlantic Hijack, but a stand-alone novel

Dancing on the Beach (978-1-78222-431-0). A romantic thriller. Achieved a most popular read category on promotekdbook.com in 2016 and in 2018.

Poems with themed notes (978-1-78222-464) An anthology of forty poems.

Galactic Mission (978-1-78222-512-6). A science fiction novel listed with previews on Amazon.

url: amazon.com/author/grantsam

Request from the author

If you enjoy reading Mists of Time, please post a short review on your bookseller's web page where you purchased the book. Similarly, short reviews on the Amazon site will also be appreciated for other novels or anthologies.

PART ONE

Poems

ROBYN HODE

"Loxley
-Earl of Loxley
may I speak with you
across the tracts of time?

The one believed to be
named - the Robyn Hode,
that owned, perhaps, a title,
- also, of Robert de Loxley

It will not matter
that you are not Saxon;
for you appear a beacon of
incandescent truth/light
for those oppressed by
powerful persons.

A medieval bandit
some say you were.
But those with
much to hide would
prefer to see that side.

Robin, Robyn Hode,
Robert de Locksley
- for in the legend
you speak still
as one who
in deeds and action inspired
true loyalty. Not bought in
power and wealth -
but then employed to confound
the injustice of harsh rulers!

Captured in story lines
of great escape
from evil of that day.

You sir, your loyal band
in ballads, memory,
talk, retain, fond recall.
You surpass forever,
the pomp and show of kings;
- transcend the world's
fast-chattering chariot of time.
Not only to win Maid Marion's love,
but warm the hearts of
the poor oppressed.

Address to historical character. Previously published in a Forward Poetry anthology.

CIRCLE OF LIFE

Small, squalling,
Needy, dependant,
Seeking attention,
meaning, reward.

Life maintained,
experience gained.
Roles re-enforced
developed, rejected?

Feelings tell
there's more.
Love for others.
We need still.

Alone sometimes,
but weaved
within that
thread of humanity.

Sometime.
Somehow.
Somewhere.
We leave.

Then, to
be with that
all powerful
love that made us.

It has grown,
while we lived.
Now we arrive
to be individual part.

This for people,
Animals, sunlit
meadows, trees,
sunrise and set.

Life on
earth, where
our heart
sang and danced.
Nothing lost.
Where good
is remembered.

EPIC POEM: MISTS OF TIME

A solitary walk down leaf-wrapped lane,
glimpse world; near lost, save now.
Unexpected presence captured, revealed;
time corridor in past.

Chimney curl of smoke;
rough-cut grass.
Fence, rambled rose.
Pans of milk,
with fresh milk, heated;
steam, merged in cold air;
await surface cream.

Boxes opened,
stacked;
eggs nestled,
kept, in weaved basket.
First found in hedge,
clumped turf, nook,
cranny-near
farm door.

Sought and taken.

Await inspection;
cleaned, sized-
then to market.

That view 'cross,
cobbled, splattered, yard;
tractor, machinery;
a tree top perch;
then rolling hills.

Stabled black colt, bolts,
with opportunity;
thro' opened door, by me.

Eyes, senses, mind, download;
sixty years absent.
No more, the people
time, nor farm.

Day, of days;
exchanged transferred.

Town life,
to isolated farm.
With routines
to maintain.

A thirteen-year old,
who baled hay;
swigged rough cider mix -
with orange, whisky.
-- Even got paid!

A smuggled time.
Exploded, capsule;
scented, sounds.
Memory, back-streamed
thro' this canopied leafed lane.

Sculpted, past.
Light streamed
in cathedral's nature.

Informed, refreshed,
in memory;

caught, re-staged;
mind revived.

Return, opened;
youth capture of
unworried world.

———————

Pre-sea, life, to follow.
Ships, crossed world.
Fast appreciation met soon.
That farm idyll?
part of life's run spool?
Interlude not imagined;
lost, now drawn back.

Teen-years, fancied
desire for women.
Young, not girls.
Pleasantries, smiles,
but no permanence,
in youth's journey

Heart dismay,
when their glow
wasn't love, but
friendliness.
Warm affection felt;
young, too young.
Slow realization.
They with same aged
boyfriend, fiancé,
soon to marry;
obvious? But not then,
for disappointed heart.

First training that-
love can disappoint;
not always retained.
That died fierce flame
in other, not now for you.
Love known, retracted-
spilt, spoilt- for other,
extinguished-
like day to night.

That-brute bravery,
is then a must;
to meet reality.
Camp sites,
will be a ship.
Then another, another,
another...

A familiar,
meet place.
Supported, dialogue.
Togetherness of
sea life share.

They, listen, understood;
related to this in others.
Not those with land-
locked, hassled life.
With daily ritual
to work and home.

First shore greets,
perhaps by these, that

foreign travel-
weeks at sea-exotic visits-
-not real work- 'gainst,
theirs of rush, dash to
pay bills.
Give family nurture.

Theirs, of felt perpetual
office, factory- cracked,
relentless whip;
demanded presence, response.
Keyboards tap make words.
Now electronic blink;
internet, text, targets, messages.
Stale air, frenzy, fug.

Minutiae of home, flat.
Roof overhead- not ship maintenance.
Wife, children responsibility,
immediacy of task in work.
Domestic need and home.

Near forgotten, are those teens.

Young years, when self- needs
outweighed much else.
Before responsibility of crew,
employee, husband, wife, provider,
who contributes beyond their self.

———————

How wilful, and unforgiving
could that sea mistress be?
When denied great respect;
prepared not for
strength in wind,
mountainous sea.

A fearful place to
be when fire broke out;
in holds or quarters;
hard to reach and quell.

Habitations of sorrow,
kaleidoscope back,
in this recall picture.
Forward trails

followed, but
incomplete in,
train memory rush.

Sequential decades tapped.
Farm, now in recall.
Shared with others.
Togetherness.
Their farm lives kept,
in long stay,
embrace.

That generator stopped.
No cows to milk.
No bulbs to light.
No electric supply;
now daylight.
Viewed, virtual,
misted form arisen
frame, this while;
green canopied lane.

Walk, but no distance,
for fear-
that this clear tapestry,
will bubble pictures;
away to still air.

That, yesterday.
Two collie dogs sat.
Yet jumped, to greet, lick, hands, legs.
Far too, friendly, tamed, spoilt,
by me and all,
to work the sheep.

There to stroke each,
its head, neck, back, sides;
yet preference shown
slighted other in a whimper.
So fair and true were these.

Remembered - pears;
clumped, in bowl;
laid to ripen.
Purchased week previous,

at market show.
Pigs, sheep, cattle,
orchard produce.

Livestock auctioneer,
was seen to duck,
not that hidden, by trailer;
-glugged whisky, bottle swigs.
Dutch courage or just plain addiction?

Neighbours, friends
joined by wedding.
Evening meal.
Cutlery, plates,
electric carving knife;
gifted-then in use.

A matchbox slice
of cake to take;
for distant relatives,
-all those there we meet.
Share in couples joy.

Fresh, my eyes to see.
Felt, happiness,
warm friendship;
gathered harvest.
Two celebrations.

That world caught back
along this walked lane.

———————

Then transferred to storm
tossed sea;
look out; watches;
holy stoned decks.
Goggles worn to chip
paint, underlying rust;
red leaded; undercoat then gloss.
Green stained brass to rub;
polish mirror clean.
Wheelhouse decks to scrub.

Navigation, seamanship,
Ship construction, science,

English, maths -all to study.
Stapled, chaptered, course sheets.
Grapple to complete- return to marker.
---Not finished all- by college-tutor, time.
Test papers;
the Second Mate's exam.

Sea return, then followed.
- to pace that wheelhouse, bridge.
First, a tanker kept in Middle/
East lands.
Far out from British
Strike bound ports.

Visited by raging fire;
Red Sea, east of Suez.
Crew and ship survived.
Destination Japan.

Ore carriers, cargo liners,
then departure made,
from sea experience,
hatched in sea cadet.

Time ashore for study.
Away from all ships and sea.
Not in contemplative
leafed lanes;
but libraries,
colleges, lodgings/ flats.

Out of sea life;
more varied subjects.
Opposite sex
to distract.

Work found in hotels,
Restaurants. But----
new industrial strike arrived.
Hotel workers;
union, members met.
Gathered to listen
on beach front.

"More pay, more pay!"
-strike threat ended;
--employers gave

fifteen pound.
For new waiter's week.

Romance arrived;
took control.
Snatched that away;
new found love.

A magic spell.
Within a year
-broken, snapped,
separated, unglued,
-the two of us.

Wounds licked,
Then it was,
to sea front beaches,
promenades, holiday makers;
deck chair attendant role

Shared laughter, fun, glee.
A revolved door with swap
for new holidaymakers,

in those summer weeks.
This season break;
then career to find.

Interviews, appointments;
- enthusiastic talk,
about company
hardly known;
but in excited tone,
you parade,
history to impress.

No more now
Sea, ships,
deck chairs;
new venture-
bank branch official,
just outside City.

Lonesome malaise,
Stifled in offices.
Frazzled by courses.
No sign of bank crash,

but notice given.

Return to;
season with
sun, wind, salted air;
breeze flapped
deck chairs
beckoned;
before return to
new search for
interviews/ career.

Application made.
Rewarded with
several invitations.
-Interviewer excited.
A first meet with
trained lifeboatman.

Perhaps with skill
that might
arrest retail
sinking sales?

Arenas of experience: -
office, personnel, restaurant,
fashion, food, sweets, cosmetics, clocks,
household goods, shoes, hats, leather goods, toys
luggage, curtains, lighting.
Fifty- four departments.

Ports of the world,
exchanged for
town and city stores;
plans- to complete.
Expressed in percentage.
weekly figures – "this week,"
"last week, against "last year."
How much individual weekly sale?
In apples, dresses, curtains,
pork pies or bread?
A manager's store sale plan,
prepared with slide rule.

Store retail life.
With floor extensions
further growth;

others need rescue plans,
in towns where no work.

Later, retail life in
city centres lost appeal.
Notice then given.
Unemployment beckoned.

Chimed with others
before and since;
start of postal work;
paid a rent;
tabled food.

Thirty years
of Xmas post.
Did lead to walks,
in leaf, strewn lane;
pavements, roads.

Towns, village streets.
Postal bags to fill;
trains to meet, collect

and make dispatch.

Retired from post;
those cycle rides-
articulated feet and hands-
weight filled pouches.
Individual memory
stayed, but no longer
life-filled-work.

Farm, sea,
deck chairs, hotels, restaurant,
bank branch retail
then mainly postal.

Re-ignite of retail,
when shops were
designed, constructed
by eldest son.

Cabinets, revolved;
Parker, Cross and
Sheaffer pen.

Leather organizer
plus, new pen;
to be bought
for colleague;
farewell gift.

Felt tip, marker, calligraphy,
propelling pencils.
Dump bins filled.
Biros, pencils five-a-pound.

Print paper 100gm.
Stacked in wells;
to catch window-watcher,
paper eaters.

Collins Diaries,
annual planners.
A4, A5, diary, pocket.
Five year all in one.

Hard backed books.
Lined or not.

Accounts, sketch,
exercise, graph,
squared, and plain.

Kodak photo,
Print paper, wedding cards.
Ink cartridge, multi coloured;
not just black.

Art brush, paints.
Small, medium, large canvas.
Easel, palettes,
chalk, crayon.
Portfolio holders.
Paint by numbers.

Decorative spinners.
Multi-card with envelope.
Coloured card and paper,
to give card makers
their taste of heaven.

New merchandise.
Manager, work force
to select and train.
Unwrapped retail skill.
Stores attracted
good sales.

Familiar territory,
although, locked apart
When engaged
in postal work.

Swirled memory mist,
now met in walk,
through, canopied, leafed lane.

BREAKING FREE, IMAGINED INTERLUDE

Waves, rhythmically,
break a silence
with arrival
on the shore.

Roses, part budded;
others already open,
scent, invigorate the air.

Hanging baskets, fresh in bloom;
where summer
is forever,
no other season known.

Gardens, reach back.
Flowers bloom and produce ripens.
There streams flow down
snow-capped mountains,
to fill a crystal lake.

An idyll, which
invigorates, body,
spirit, soul.

Captured at present time,
understood by all.
To greet, those before
and now returned.

Befriended, loved.
Shared appreciation,
in this pastoral/
sea/ mountain/ home.

Senses very sharp.
New memory is to make.
Brief interlude.
And good
intentions meet,
generously guided spirit.
With this imagined visit.

Beach idyll and
Eden garden view.

Shared memory;
released knowledge.
Hidden when apart.
Hopes, dreams,
worked through or not?
In each our own life's throw.

An imaginary place,
we cannot stay.

life ever needs
renewal;
sustained by
beating hearts.

Together we
return.

Chosen for Forward Poetry anthology.

ETERNAL LOVE: AN INVITATION

Eternal love invites,
insists a presence;
more than just a glimpse.

An entrance made in
prairies of the mind;
to lift a heart.

Another's eyes
expressing care;
a voice beloved.

Words or music;
that caress retained;
and new memory.

Nature's voice;
that harmonizes;
but has ruthless strength.

Eternal, rhythm;
- sunrise, morning;
evening, night.

To caress,
that inner being;
which feels, sees;
eternal love.

Published by Forward Poetry in 2017.

FUN IN THE SUN
SEA, PEBBLES, SAND

Galloping waves,
salt stung eyes;
heat smacked feet;
baked sand.

Young voices
shape the air.
Glee filled delight
at seaside fare.

Deep blue sea;
waves beat to shore;
rhythmic pattern;
bubbled surf.

Slivered seaweed;
rock pool finds;
bucket spaded,
castles built.

Last dash;
final swim.
Next day,
again, the same.

Waves beat
constant rhythm,
falling, rising
on the sand.

Young voices
shape the air.
Glee smiled delight
at nature's fare.

Photos of each
taken on the beach
treasured in
later winter months.

Sand scooped castle
meets the tide.
Seaweed decorates
new daily, build.

From rock pool
then to
castle wall.

Forward Poetry Anthology, 2018 publication.

LIGHT AND DARKNESS

Light
gives colour
out of dark.

Light
takes seed
to plant.

Light
persuades
bud to open.

Dark
makes life
retreat

Dark
hides
from the light.

Dark
understands
not the light.

Chosen for anthology, in 2017. Light and Dark. By Forward Poetry

FREE YOUR MIND: FREEDOM IS A SKATEBOARD

A first ollie
gives lift:
skateboard
dances; turns; twists;
body; muscles; arms; legs; feet.

It's freedom
with practice to gain control;
no needed dependence
on another persons' skill.

Carve; heel flip; kickflip;
I master these and
fakie; backside;
broadside; frontside.

Each practice
acquires more skill.
A forward adventure,

to control at will,
fast rolled wheels.

Tailside; tic tac;
varial heel flip;
kickflip; increase
my freedom from fall.
Perseverance,
practice, evolving skill.

Freedom is a
Skateboard
Freed to
be part with me.
Skate board skills.
Performed at my will.

Scheduled for publication 31st July, 2018. Forward Poetry.

THEY GAVE ALL

Nations,
resisted
tyrant rule.

In a unity,
they fought,
to regain, and
save their lands.

Unknown horror,
yet to face:
battlefield, trench,
torpedo, bomb, shell.

Each,
final-breath,
they gave-
our light,
freedom.

Pneumonia,
training accidents,
snatched lives;
billeted in dank tents;
not yet in war.
These also gave
for us,
today's light,
and freedom.

Torpedoed, bombed,
Shelled, mined.
Merchant ships,
brought supplies.

Many lives drowned, lost.
Not even a fighting force!

They also gave for us
today's light and freedom.

Captured forces.
Captors that brutalized;
enslaved, starved; worked to
death, in torture camp; those,
no longer combatants.

Not wanting to talk,
of suffering -
horrific gruesome,
bestial, barbaric- this
memory, preferred shut out.

Lives taken,
in many thousands.

Honour, always, forever;
we must give
their lives.

We see clearly
wars futility,
but, they gave all.

Today,
life's gift
marches from this
fight for freedom.

Lives torn away;
on land, sea-
in barbaric-
war-torn sky.

Humility, humility,
draw, deep, deep breath,
in remembrance;
love for these,
who made escape to
freedom possible -not, enslavement.

To live freely.
For they gave all.

Hold close
in hearts and minds,
memory, always,
for those who
went to war-
to fight- to free.

Let's seek not
enmity, but peace-
across the world,
they left- but gave all.

"Darkness Falls"- Forward Poetry. Scheduled anthology, for 2018

FINANCIAL PICTURE BOOK

The image of financial cliffs, tipping points,
quantitative easing, invisible earnings,
run on the bank;
catch phrases from that City song book

-that can fearfully frighten
the innocent bingo player;

not the economist or polemicist
-wanted another-ist.

How can bread and cheese be found, let alone
fresh-filled scones, fancy gateaux and other delicacies,
when trillion of debt feast on tomorrow's
yeast - nowhere near, the flour and oven?

A time when the portrait was of trees
festooned with blossom abundant.
Harvested by we, the worker bees, dodging back and forth -
on trains – computing – feverishly - on phone and laptop
to meet that deadline,

before dark strangles out any light.

To tip, and tap, on lap top.
Devise Nirvana with new plan.
Ducking, diving, pushing, shoving,
before we're trapped,
in some frantic scramble.
Fallen in dark labyrinth.
Dipping, diving, running, planning, loving.
Finding work in that other market,
that serves demand - not those stalls of fruit and veg.

Has a king not paid his rent with talk of sovereign debt?
How does a mountaineer start to climb a fiscal cliff??
or has that base camp party never ended???

It's all perplexing when it turns to metaphor, that blurs the truth.
No clear concise plan to show, how
the wheels on the bus take us back to plus!

Published in "Unlocked," A Frome Writers Collective anthology, 2018.

SLEEP DEPARTS MEMORY BRINGS FORWARD THE FUTURE

Perfume pricked the
shallow receptors
of my waking thoughts.
Wrenched and dragged
me out of drugged state.
Back to that delight of
remembered sensual
pleasure.

Sound sense arrived
from...
pattering shower spray.

That enervated
aquiline form;
sponge soaping
each raised leg.
Happiness in

coal-black eyes
that seek and find;
to give...
loves darted smile.

Kiss formed lips
then caress my
inner-being.

A glimpse of that
future happiness
perhaps, together;
merged with eternity.

SUMMER INTRUDER

Flecks of dancing light
dapple mark the lane.
Diamond water sparkle
flickers on the dew.
The clicking
metal lever,
kicks open the
four-barred gate.

Then out the valley's depth
an animal like roar,
scatters birds from hedgerows
on this sunny summer day.

Its powerful breath
Takes hostage all, quiet and peace.
Holding a giant paw on
the wide-open gate.

A lone dog
howls in protest

at nature's
fierce intruder.

Slates ripped
away, like cards, shuffled in a pack.
Drop and smash in gardens,
from houses in its track.

Flayed beech and
cherry leaf lies,
torn from living- branch;
scattered on the road.

Flecks of dancing light
dapple mark the lane.
Diamond water sparkle
flickers on the dew.

Published in "Unlocked," a Frome Writers Collective anthology for 2018.

WE MEET-WE PART-WE MEET

A smile,
sweet recognition.
We meet.
We talk.

'Today, they've
locked you out?'
'Appointments? - "yes,"
but without names.'

"You have to guess,
whose next;"
time placed, listed,
with no patient name.

Distant in years,
though you share;
admire your acceptance
balance and calm.
A download that's failed.

Scales will tell!
Don't disappoint!
Weeks passed;
need weight loss!

Banned sweet biscuits,
unnecessary cake;
---walked more: occasional
-but measured drink.

Flow of calories
much reduced.
Seventy grams, no more
in that sweet, yoghurt, pot.

Healthy eating!
+ exercise is good-yes!
Sensible ingredients, advised.
Your tact, charm, beauty,
give added reason to be living.

Chosen for publication by Forward Poetry.
But Author missed edit date submission, 2018.

WINTER LIKE LOATHE?

NOT FOREVER...

Spiky trees
inhabit skylines;
vibrant green leaves
snatched from branch
by rain, cold and wind.

Multi-membraned life form
that once built canopies
with green lattice spread.

Birthed -not yet a year.
But now all are dead.

Leaf's decayed, skeletal
remains...
forgotten on a
forest floor.

Crinkled in the
ice cold ground.

Or trapped in a
gully to...
swirl with other
blackened leaves.

Consumed by winter's
scavenge of summer's
unique show.

But the winter solstice
means day can stay
longer in the fight.

Buds decide
to open;
yellow shoots catch
a colour.

Mind's anxious
dread of winter
soothed by spring's
caress.

Forward Poetry anthology
"About the seasons,"-publication.

CHAMPIONSHIP WEEK

Serious, intermediate,
beginners too---
meet to compete
for the week.

Locust like swarm,
sail carpets sea;
each wants first
-past that marker flag.

"Ten minutes."
Wait for gun!
Boats spin, turn;
timing is all.

Sheets flap—
--must slow down
--speed- too fast
--will cross line.

Too soon- too soon.

Like scythed grass,
many booms flip back;
to make advance again.

Puffed smoke;
cliff echoes gun;
free to start-
-go, go, go.

Each race leg advance,
tests individual crew.
Close haul skill;
reach and run.

Leader group
can be caught- if
trailed boats,
meet new breeze.

Crews which sail
these local waters,
will know
-that sneaky tide!

Strong winds,
rough seas-help
"weighty," crew;
lighter winds favour others.

Each day,
skill the premium.
Last year's winner;
on his/her mettle.

capsizes, collision,
rigging tangled,
rules broken;
leads some to disqualify.

Cup winner need
not finish...
first each day, but
ends in table lead.

Race boat crews,'
might do better.
- very encouraged

-now, in first hundred!

Others- escape.
Holiday, break-
be with dinghy tribe,
sail, socialize.

Forward Poetry's -summer of sport.
Entry 28th August, 2018.

LIMERICK: ALPINE LOVE

There was a young man from France
who learnt to yodel and dance?
To impress a Swiss girl
he'd met in the alps
who wanted to do more than just Karaoke.

Chosen for poetry style genre anthology: Forward Poetry.

PART TWO

Short Stories

MARS LANDING WITH UPGRADE FOR SCOTT

{extract from science fiction novel}

'Ivor, we have food and oxygen from rapid growth leaf vines. The chemical interaction between inner and outer globes generates light and charges our battery supply, but we have lost contact with earth transmissions-and you, you say you are not worried? Said Scott.

'There is food to feed a spaceship crew. Our telescopes can explore and pick up signals from beyond the solar system. Pah! You Americans are so earth trapped. 'You whimper- "I miss the coke and ice cream, and the adverts to buy yet more crap on media channels." - you say this. I can only say how can you not wonder at the beauty of the view of other planets and the flow of signals that are picked up from other systems that are all but hidden from earth?'

'Easily, Ivor, because I was trained to bring the ship here. I was to assist in the landing of supplies and people into this Martian capsule and then to leave. I brought you to assist with the operation of the automata. Then the Captain radios down that there's an intergalactic storm heading toward Mars, leaves the shuttle outside with us here and vamooses. You were there with me and you are in the programme I am not! I never volunteered for a planet camp.

'Okay, okay, calm down. Passengers are delayed by hold ups at space stations on route to the moon or other earth orbiting holiday destinations.'

'Yes, but they are in civilized communal living spaces. Also, there are flights back to earth every few hours. There are no flights to anywhere here on Mars. Not on this side. This is the industrial side and space mineral ships arrive only twice a year They're manned by automata pilot and crew. We're the only humans in this cultivation bubble sphere. Cultivation bubble, that's a joke. Not really for human habitation- more a farm for creepy crawly insects, bee colonies and plants distorted by genetic modification to produce pollen all year around.

'It's as I said, you are very parochial.'

'Parochial, because I prefer life on earth to life in a super resolution Mars capsule! You astound me.'

'Maybe, Scott, but perhaps it is a good thing that we are like opposites. Perhaps in the next month when an automaton builds a replica replacement, you can describe the various obstacles that were overcome to achieve self-replication. You might find the biological genetic code build for plant proliferation, equally intriguing. I studied early research into this development on earth.'

'What is that large box with hatches to do with plants?'

Scott pointed to a large tank sized box.

'There was a drop from an orbiting ship that visited one of Jupiter's moons. It's an automaton upgrade.' A large black box with tripod legs now relaxed to allow the box to rest, in the left far corner of the capsule, behind the Alpine styled chalet. Mars capsules were known as cathedrals, due to their vast height, which allowed large structures to be built and storage facility.'

Ivor, zapped for a human Mars habitability report from the newly arrived capsule. A screen projection appeared in front of them with a script which read – "Organic and animal life can now enjoy inhalation of oxygen with the protection of cloud cover."

Amazingly Scott said. 'I might stay, with all this outdoor space.'

THE MANOR HOUSE

Rivulets, streamed down tree trunks, breaking into a quiet, decayed, stillness of that wood. Ravaged elm trees, forlorn, like some bombed out town. I walked towards the Manor House. I'd asked at the station about accommodation.

"Phone Mrs Batchem, at the Manor, she takes in guests-minding it for the Colonel, she is. There's nowt else here for bed and breakfast," said the ticket collector at Ucklesbury station. I enquired on my mobile from Dunroamin cottage. This particular deceased client's inventory would need time to complete "That's quite right, but you won't mind the grand- children. They'll be a-bed afore you, no doubt," said Mrs Batchem. I booked there and then. The bank would reimburse. Once out of the dead elm forest, the three-storey Manor loomed in front. The word Manor twinned with House on the adjacent gate post.

Rain from guttering, tumbled into the garden. I tugged the oval metal handle, making the bell clang repeatedly. Bolts thudded, the door caught on a chain. I leant forward and said,

'It's Mr Stevens. I booked earlier.

'Mr Stevens, I've been expecting you.' A pointed nose retreated. The door bolt released. I was the first to speak.

'It's very good to put me up at short notice. It's a filthy evening.'

'That's quite all right. Maurice from the station, let me know, you would be wanting - bed and breakfast,' she said, and fully opened the door. Mrs Batchem wore a navy skirt, matching coat and white blouse. Long black hair teamed up with hooped golden ear rings. She smiled.

'Do come in, won't you?

Lines around her eyes merged with prettily etched cheeks. Friendly and welcoming. I guess mid- forties.

'There's a fire in the drawing room. The Colonel never lights the fire, except for guests. You'd like tea and sandwiches, perhaps? Cheese and chutney or just plain cheese?

'Cheese and chutney-that sounds good.' I had downed a pie and pint at the White Hart, not expecting food, but pleased to be offered tea and sandwiches.

'I'll show you your room Mr Stevens. The bath rooms opposite. We'd best go quietly-the grand children are asleep.' I followed her upstairs. She turned the Yale key in the bedroom door, removed it and gave it to me. I walked over and placed my suitcase and laptop on a high-backed chair by the bedroom window. A double room with wardrobe, chest of drawers. Two silver candle sticks stood on a mantelpiece facing a double bed.

'Fifteen minutes and I'll have the tea and sandwiches

ready.' She smiled and closed the door.

A blood red wallpaper was disturbed more than decorated with pictures of the highlands. Above the mantelpiece there was the imprint from a long slim object, which had been removed, leaving a darker redness. I considered asking about this, but Mrs Batchem did most of the talking

'How very interesting, Miss Simkins used to visit the shop for a quarter of hum-bugs, every week. I help at the post office occasionally. But she didn't stop by a few weeks back. Died in the garden, she did. The postman couldn't get an answer. He told us, there was a parcel and he'd try the following day. He still couldn't get an answer. Sal, the postmistress first phoned the doctor. He called the police after there was no reply. They smashed the door open with a crow bar. Found her in the back garden. Shears were locked in a branch, and she was lay on the ground. A keen gardener, you see. Died doing what she liked doing, you might say.'

'That explains the new set of keys the bank gave me,' I said. I considered that I might as well explain why I was in Ucklesbury. It wasn't a state secret that I did bank inventories for deceased clients with no living relatives.

'I've to get the grand children's clothes ready, you'll have to excuse me. The remotes by the TV and there's the Ucklesbury Times if you are wanting some local news.'

'Thanks Mrs Batchem.' The carriage clock, stridently interrupted, before I continued.

'I started early from Paddington. I won't be long for bed- I wonder, is there a broadband connection by any chance?'

'Yes, the Colonel's very into IT. There's a card behind the clock. I got up and removed a calling type car.

'Be sure to replace it, won't you? I do breakfast for eight-thirty. A full English is that all right?'

'That's great, Mrs Batchem.'

'Will you be wanting tea or coffee Mr Stevens, which would you prefer, tea or coffee?' She was standing.

'There's orange juice.'

'Black coffee will be fine,' I said.

'Will you be needing a call?'

'No, it's okay, I'll set my phone to wake me.'

'Modern technology does so much now, doesn't it? She replied. 'I'll wish you a good night's sleep then.'

I messaged the bank with an update on progress. My eyes closed momentarily, long enough to startle me on waking, expecting to see the furniture of my own lounge. It was definitely time for bed!

A walk upstairs, removed the sleep drug effect. I brushed my teeth in the bath room. Once in bed I accessed photos from Abbie. They were sent from the Norwegian fjords aboard a cruise ship. We'd met on a bank course. I asked her out on my thirty-ninth birthday. Last week, I turned forty. An instant attraction. She insisted it cooled. Although separated from her husband she wanted the divorce to be finalized. I was comforted to see that in the selfies the photos featured just her and Millie, a former school friend. Mainly the two of them with scenic views of the fjords as a back drop- it was no good, I needed sleep and connected the I-pad to a charger. Returned to bed and set my phone to give a jingle at seven forty-five. The old feathery type mattress, wrapped itself around me.

I was dreaming, when I first realized that there was someone or something in the room, I felt to be awake. That was the strangeness. I was aware of being unable to move, lay on my back, but managed to move my arms, backwards in the dream, to raise my back.

At the front of the black mantelpiece, in my dream state, a young woman, appeared, in a pocketed tartan cape, over a white night dress. Candles flickered at each end of the mantle piece. Black tresses curled around her shoulders and a white night dress highlighted her hair. Above the mantelpiece that strip of bright red wallpaper now covered with a dirk in its scabbard. I was attracted by the raw beauty, but her face was one of anger. I could see the whites of her eyes around the coal black sparkle of the pupils, seeking recognition. A look, full of anger, directed towards me. Yes, I now know, it surely was only a dream but I felt the full force of her wrath. Frozen with fear and trapped in a dream capture.

She turned, withdrew the dirk from its scabbard. I heard myself scream from a searing pain in my stomach, as she lunged forward. A cockerel crowed from a nearby farm which made anger turn to disappointment on her face. Pressure of the dirk in my flesh went and her life size figure shrank. It seemed to fade back into the mantle piece. Now awake; equally captivated by the ravishing beauty of the young woman and terrified at the same time.

'You, can't have my phone to play games on, it's not my fault you left yours on

charge at home.'

'Gran isn't she mean. Sara's not using her phone. It's upstairs in the bedroom

'When you've finished breakfast, you can both go into the orchard and play clock golf. Your mother's picking you up soon. It'll be your last chance.' It went quiet and the green baize door opened moments later. Mrs Batchem carried my breakfast in on tray.

'Did you sleep well Mr Stevens? I meant to ask.' I wasn't sure whether the grand children were in hearing range and said,

'I went to sleep straightaway.'

'Dunroamin cottage's nearby,' She placed the tray on the sideboard.

'Yes, that's fortunate. Although it would be nice if the rain stopped.

'Is the manor old?' She placed my breakfast down and went to fetch the tray with the coffee from the side board.

'I should say so. Built 1815, just after the Battle of Waterloo.'

'Old enough to produce a ghost I would imagine.' I was fishing to discover more.

'There's Annie MacBride. But I've neither seen nor heard her. My grandchildren-you know children-Mr Stevens, they have wild imaginations. They've said that they've heard footsteps across the landing. Young Sara has said she saw a young woman in a tartan cape and night dress when she came down to get her phone. They watch so many films. It's all in their imagination, I'm sure. I've not told them the story, though about Annie. The Colonel, said there was the ghost, called Annie before he left. I do wish he hadn't. That started them off. Any unusual noise they've since heard has been Annie! It's all in their minds, Mr Stevens.'

'What do you know about Annie, Mrs Batchem?' I heard a scream from the kitchen.

'You dare, Justin. Give me back that charger.'

'Perhaps, after breakfast, I can tell you more. Sara and

Justin need keeping an eye on. That's if you don't mind joining me around the kitchen table. I'll need to watch them from there

'Yes, I'd like that,' I said. She smiled and left for the kitchen.

'You two! Justin give Sara her charger and both of you can put your shoes on and play in the orchard for half an hour.' I later carried the tray from the dining room to the kitchen.

I placed the tray on the kitchen table. A square oak table with the end leaves down.

'Thank you. Do sit down, won't you,' she said. I sat opposite. Not an elaborate kitchen. The ivory painted walls were cupboarded both sides of the Aga, which was built into an inglenook, beneath a large mantle piece. A faded portrait of a young woman in fine clothes looked down. The eyes looked familiar. Both, washing machine and dish washer seemed somehow futuristic beneath a drying frame that hung from the ceiling.

'I don't have many guests. It's nice talking with the outside world, you might say.' Mrs Batchem, sipped her tea, elbows on table.

'I'm Alice- an old-fashioned name. Alice was the name of mother's favourite teacher.'

'Brandon.' I said. There was a Canadian great uncle on my father's side with that name. I was called All Bran at school.' She smiled, perhaps in memory of her schooldays. I'd ventured pass the threshold of just a paying guest. Alice continued by telling me about Marge or Margie, the previous housekeeper. A boisterous individual, who apparently gave womanly advice to the Colonel, but winkled out of him the connection of Annie Mac Bride with the Manor. Then, his wife left him for a younger man, and Alice said that Marge made it clear that unless he found another wife she would leave, also.

'And did he?' I asked Alice, who told me that he wasn't making much progress until Marge got him on a dating website. I then asked whether Marge was interested. Alice laughed and said that she wouldn't be - not with a female partner! But Marge, Alice said, wasn't impressed with his choice of women. He wanted to date single mothers with children. Alice, was surprised that any young woman would want him, but she said that next month he was going on a family outing to Alton Towers with a woman called Anita, and her two children. Marge said that she decided to leave, because she couldn't stand children. That didn't seem to bother Alice. Now that her daughter's children were at school, she would see less of them and didn't mind it if there were children at the manor. I wanted to know more about Annie. According to Alice there were only rumours about her, before Marge got the story out of the Colonel.

Annie, apparently travelled down from Scotland with her Laird, in eighteen ninety. The Laird then, was great uncle to the Colonel. There was a coachman, but no other servants. The Laird's wife died, and he acquired a mistress. Annie was her maid servant and the Laird fell for her and she for him. Annie arrived at the Manor, first as his maid servant. Alice said, that she would have been like his chattel or property. Marge, Alice said, was of the belief that it would not have been a love match, but just plain lust for a younger woman. The Manor House was his English retreat and staffed with servants, who awaited their Laird's appearance. With Annie, in servants' dress, the Laird gathered the staff and told them that Annie MacBride was to be their new mistress. Fine clothes were bought. She liked to wear tartan, a statement of her Highland ancestry. That it was likely to have been difficult for Annie. Romantic attachment to their Laird, would have upset staff at the manor. A maid servant becoming the mistress! I asked Alice whether they did get married.

That was planned to take place. Alice, said that according to Marge Annie took to the wearing of an engagement ring. The Colonel said, it was afterwards given to his mistress. I questioned the fact that the Laird would want to marry a servant girl, but apparently, he did. A letter arrived, continued Alice, stating that she wanted him to return to Scotland. Annie was to stay at the Manor. The mistress now had a new maid servant. But, of course knew nothing of how Annie was bride to be. Alice then said how tragic it was with the name Mac Bride, but also that it was believed that Annie read the message beforehand. When he told her that he would return to the Highlands on business, she questioned this. They argued. It was said the servants over-heard the two rowing, but the coach man was told to prepare the coach and horses. Marge told Alice that the Colonel told her that there was a great stillness in the house and that the moon became red in the sky. I asked what happened and this is what Alice said.

'That the details are still not fully known, but the coach man drove the coach from the coach house around, and into the drive way early that next morning. The Laird's belongings were packed and he said that they would stop and breakfast at The Old Red Lion in Tewkesbury.'

'Was it the main entrance where it says -Manor House?' I asked.

'Yes, that would be it,' she replied. Alice continued,

'Then when the coach was near to the entrance the horses reared up. It was near to dawn. He reined them in and got down and there face down on the cobbles was Annie. It is said that there was blood down her night dress, but that she was breathing. He opened the coach door picked her up and placed her inside. Then went to waken the then housekeeper. Immediately she saw Annie in the coach, she said to take her to the hospital. There being so much blood. And that she would stay in the coach with her.' Alice face whitened as she recalled the story, but continued,

'The coachman it was said recalled that there was a terrible moaning from Annie. Her head was bloodied and once at the hospital they got help to take her inside. The two of them waited by the coach and shortly afterwards a doctor with two nurses came out and said that she died in their arms. When back at the manor, it was decided that the coach man, should go to the Lairds bedroom to wake him. He was met with the horrendous sight of the Laird lay across the bed with a dirk in his middle. The sash window was wide open and each curtain with blood hand prints.' I wanted to know more about the Laird, but Alice, Mrs Batchem continued.

'Evidently if Annie couldn't have him neither would the mistress. At an inquest a coroner determined death by suicide, whilst her mind was disturbed, for poor Annie. It was a double-edged dirk. Marge, could have left the gory details out, but it was his blood on the nightdress. There was blood and more in the pockets of the cape. That blow to the head could have killed her, but it was not that severe and actual cause of death was listed as heart failure. Margie, said that Annie's ghost might be expected, given the tragic circumstances, but she said no woman ever sees her ghostly form. That's why I don't believe that she's appeared to Sara. The Colonel's in his eighties, but he's never seen nor heard anything that might be Annie's ghost. He just jokes about it. You might say that it's no more than a story. It wouldn't surprise me if it was all made up. It might be made up by the Colonel perhaps to keep Margie on her toes, who knows?

'How old was the Laird, when he died Alice? Was that mentioned?

'Not that old. He was about forty. There's a portrait of him in the Colonel's private living room.

'Might I have a look, at the painting?'

'Don't suppose there'd be harm in that. When he's away it's kept locked. Just a quick in and out, mind. The portrait's over the mantlepiece.'

'Like the dirk was before?'

'Suppose it is when you think about it,' she said. Alice went to a frosted glass key cabinet, unlocked it and removed a bundle of keys. I could make out the word "Colonel" on the tab, which was polished brass with serrations across the bottom, like you see on a book mark. We walked out of the kitchen through the hall to an oak panelled door on the far side. Alice slid the key into the lock by the handle and opened the door. Then switched on the light.

'By the left of the mantlepiece there's a switch for

the portrait light.' I walked in and saw the picture frame above the mantlepiece. Alice remained standing in the doorway.

I pressed the switch by the mantlepiece and was startled because the light revealed a full-length portrait of a man in a frock coat with long white hair. Hair possibly a wig. A commanding presence with a hunting dog sat on one side. He held a gold topped cane in his right hand. It made you feel that he might just walk into the room even though long dead! Underneath, a plaque at the bottom of a faded gold frame. It stated:

"Laird Alistair Maclean. Born January 21st 1850. Died 7th February 1890, in tragic circumstances. Previously engaged to Annie MacBride."

There was no mention that Annie killed him.

I was myself born on 21st January and forty years old. The thought made me shiver and I felt hairs rise on my neck with the realization that I was, in fact, the same age as the deceased Laird Alistair Maclean.

{A reading was given by the author to Frome Writers scary story listeners.}

ATLANTIC HIJACK

{extract from novel}

I stood behind the wheel at eight-fifteen, only to be sent below by the Third Mate.

'Assistance with a crew member's luggage is needed by the gangway.' he said in a superior manner, before disappearing into the chart room like some high ranking official. When I stepped out on to the embarkation deck Tom was there.

'You took your time,' he said, as if I'd taken a break on my way down from the bridge.

The crew member, was tall and assured looking in a dark overcoat holding an official looking suitcase. He smiled. At that first meeting I got a sense that this was someone attempting to blend into a new role. Tall with an assurance of a person, capable of leading more than being led.

'Good of you two to give us a hand,' he said, before taking a final draught on his cigarette. He knelt and stubbed it out in the sand of a nearby fire bucket.

'That's all right, welcome aboard,' I responded.

'Fraid it's a little on the heavy side.' He pointed to a black tin trunk at the foot of the gangway.

'Two of us should be able to manage. Your cabin's

down the corridor from us, next deck up,' said Tom.

'Who is he Tom?' I asked, as our feet rattled the rungs on the gangway down to the dock.

'The new Third Engineer.'

'A replacement for Christina's dad?'

'You've got it, there's your answer.'

It was and it wasn't, because he seemed unlike the previous Third or other engineers on board, but I said nothing to Tom at the time. A figure in scarf, car coat and kid gloves arrived at the gangway, and removed what looked like a pass from his coat pocket as we lifted the tin box.

'Cutting that a bit fine, 'he said, as he jumped on to the gangway. The hoarse peep of first one tug arriving and then another making me realize he must be the pilot. I felt the metal handle of the box cutting into my hand as we reached deck level. The bosun arrived.

'Leave that there for the stewards. You two need to be at your stations.' The new arrival turned towards us as we placed his trunk on to the deck.

'Thanks for that I know the layout of the ship. You'd best do as the bosun says.'

There was a whirring sound as the hoist began hauling the gangway up from the dock for stowing. Tom returned to assist the Second Mate at the stern and I went back to the wheelhouse.

I was on the wheel until the ship left the dock basin.

The eight to twelve watch then taking over. My next watch came around too fast. A first hour of look out a running commentary on light sightings. The Monkey island above the wheelhouse, a modern equivalent of the Crow's Nest, meant as lookout you saw masthead lights early.

'Light fifty degrees on starboard bow, 'I called down the voice pipe alerting the bridge to train binoculars on the light. It was a clear night. Frequency of ship's lights reporting, meant the hour passed quickly. The Mate on occasion made starboard alterations of course to avoid approaching North bound traffic. I assisted the Mate in taking bearings, after completion of the lookout duty. By steering 173 degrees and getting positions from the Decca Navigator at ten-minute intervals, the ship crawled back to the course line of 178, after repeated earlier alterations to avoid oncoming ships.

Albany Princess carved her way through the sea with a rolling motion. It was better being wheelman, than standing on the Monkey island, togged up to keep out the

cold. I was on the wheel from seven to eight, by which time the ship was distancingfrom

the coast on to a Great Circle course which would take us to the Cape Verde Islands for re-fuelling.

There was no moon light to lick across the sea and give shadowy vision, of hatches and fore deck as I made small repeated adjustments to keep on course. The Mate's cigarette no longer glowing red was the real indication that day was taking over from night. It was seven-thirty when I glanced at my watch. The minute hand appearing then stopped by forces holding back time itself, leading to an entrapped feeling of perhaps having to steer the ship into eternity.

'Good morning Mr Mate it's good to be under way again sir, Isn't it?'

Chips entered the wheelhouse to my left. He allowed his smile to pan across to where I

was standing, and removed his battered trilby when the Mate replied.

'Good morning Chips.'

'Two new crew members this trip Mr Mate. Two young women. Company for the young apprentices, perhaps?'

'They're crew members Chippy no different from anyone else. Well that's not quite true. The fair haired girl is the Captain's daughter.'

'Really, is that so Mr Mate, 'exclaimed Chips. I could see from his surprised look, that he genuinely did not know.

'Yes, it has been decided, 'said the Mate, pausing, 'that the crew are not to be informed of the relationship. The information is that she's visiting her mother in Buenos Aires. Captain Anderson and Mrs Anderson decided that it is better that the crew are not told about the relationship.

That she blends in as a crew member. You, the Bosun and officers will be aware of the situation, but not the lower deck and boiler room ratings.'

I wasn't at the time convinced that this could be affected, without it leaking out that Jane was actually Captain Anderson's daughter.

'I understand Mr Mate. I will tell no one, said Chips. He turned to me and said,

'You boys understand this?' I nodded my head in agreement.

'Yes, she is called Miss Jane Taylor, when anyone asks.'

'I completely understand Mr Mate,' said Chips. Although, I didn't see where this

understanding was coming from, knowing the gossipy nature of Angelo about all and sundry.

'I will tell no one- nor should you,' he said again turning towards me

implicating me in the decision.

'Miss Taylor will work with the apprentices, but there is the new flag

locker that I want you to complete on the Monkey island, Chips. In the afternoons she will assist you with this when we get to warmer latitudes.' The Mate took hold of the binoculars placed on the ledge by the wheelhouse windows, pushed his glasses to his forehead and scanned the horizon from left to right. He retraced a second time to look at a passenger liner that was rapidly overhauling us on the port side. Angelo, stood just in front of me his hunched pixie like figure relaxed, over long arms at his side. The Mate, binoculars still glued to eyes, asked,

'How are you progressing with the wedging of the hatches?' Probably anticipating this question, he clasped hands together, eyes lit like someone who's discovered treasure.

'Mr Mate I've prepared the bags of wedges ready by the mastheads.'

'That's good Chips,' replied the Mate, who replaced the binoculars in their holster.

'After breakfast the apprentices and Miss Taylor can assist you with securing them in place,' said the Mate.

'I will then be on the foredeck, Mr Mate. Is that all for now Mr Mate, sir?'

'Yes Chips, but there is fresh timber, which needs preparing for shifting boards and hatches. I will talk with you tomorrow.'

'Thank you, Mr Mate, it is so good of you to give me your time sir, if that is all for now Mr Mate?'

'Yes, Chips, that is all.' It was Mr Mate this and Mr Mate that. Even "Mr Chief Mate, sir", from Angelo. For all that he was friendly and helpful to both of us apprentices.

Albany Princess at sea headed for refuel at Cape Verde Islands, 1962. Chapter describing the everyday in lead up to the hijack.

Motor Vessel *Albany Princess* is in the Atlantic. A customary visit of the Carpenter and Bosun to the Bridge, is in progress, to receive instructions from the First Mate (Chief) about the new working day. He gives instructions from the bridge, at a time when the ship is well clear of sea traffic. The wheelman will be relieved from his duty, shortly and the steering to be set on automatic pilot.

DANCING ON THE BEACH

{extract from romantic thriller}

I Didn't Immediately see Maria. Perhaps because I was hoping to see Meila. The cafeteria was in a kind of island set back from wide expanse of doors that led to offices and treatment rooms. A circular reception desk on the far side dominated the middle left wall. The lift door near a curling stairway opened which revealed a nurse and a patient in a wheel chair.

After the doors closed I looked away and saw Maria sat at a table at the outer edge of the cafeteria. Her long hair plaited and pinned up at the back, gave an Italian look. She held a cup in her hands and was viewing the flow of subtitles on the TV screen positioned on the opposite wall. She must have sensed my approach, because she put down the cup and turned.

'Hi,' I said. 'Dr Carter said you were here,' She smiled pleased perhaps to meet someone she knew in the isolating environment of the hospital. She could see I was holding a voucher in my hand.

'I'll just get in the queue – be back in a minute.' The queue now shortened to the carpeted section within the seating area. The table where Maria was sat on came into view by the time I reached the service point and the wall screen TV was showing a holiday property programme. Flat roofed villas made me guess that it might be somewhere in Spain. The caption underneath displayed a conversation between the programme presenter and prospective holiday couple. "No more sullen skies in winter. You can say goodbye to high heating bills." These words flowed across the screen. The couple were both wide-eyed when they smiled a t the camera. I could do with less heat and more air in the cafeteria. I held out the voucher to the assistant in a white cap and green overall. She took it and placed it on the steel strip behind boxes filled with beans, sausages, tomatoes, trays of bacon and fried eggs. She crossed it through with a ball point.

"Tea, coffee. Glass of orange or milk, scrambled egg on toast, bacon, egg, beans sausage or just plain cereals.' She looked enquiringly at me.

'Orange, bacon, egg and tomatoes, please,' I said. She pointed at the fruit juice cartons in the cabinet on the side and picked up a plate, in a gloved hand.

'You'll need to hand this over at the pay desk,' and passed the crossed voucher back to me.

'It's very hot,' she said with a smile and placed the breakfast plate on the tray. I slid it along the metal strips towards the cashier. After handing the voucher over I returned to where Maria was sitting.

'Thanks for waiting Maria,' I said and placed the tray

on the table with my back to the TV screen.

'I was in Out Patients,' she said. An appointment was made for me to see Dr Carter, who asked about the boat accident and the barbeque. I said it was organized by some of the deck chair attendants and then she mentioned your name. That you were in the hospital and could I wait, while you were given a blood pressure check.'

'I've still got to have that - after breakfast. And then rather unkindly, I said.

'You needn't've. It's just routine.' I didn't mention the episode that followed after I left the bench. That I was found incoherent on a park bench. Thinking back the police could have decided I was the worse for wear from drink. The hospital decided otherwise, but after an ECG scan and blood pressure check I was hopeful that they would arrive at the same conclusion as the police. I didn't tell Maria about any of this.

'No, I wanted to see you anyway, Phil. Eat your breakfast before it gets cold.'

'What about you?' I said picking up the knife and fork.

'It's eleven o'clock. I ate before I came here. My appointment was for ten.'

'With Dr Carter?'

'Yes,' I noted the pencilled eyebrows and the pinkish lipstick. A cluster of freckles either side of her eyes, which intriguingly moved together when she smiled. I tore open first one sachet of tomato ketchup and squeezed the contents on to the bacon and then the other. She screwed up her nose obviously no fan of tomato ketchup.

'It never shines like that when I'm there,' she said. I turned and saw on the screen a blue expanse of water and a white walled cottage.

'It's Galway Bay.'

'It's very pretty,' I said,' but. I guess you're here because there're more visitors and more going on.'

'Yes, and no.' I'm here to find out more about Alfie. Bit I need to get work to get by. You know employers see us Irish girls, as from a quaint Irish village, where all we do is work in pubs or cafes and help with the potato harvest.'

'That' an old-fashioned stereotype,' I said.

'You'd be surprised then if I told you that the manager's first words at the Cliff Side were-

"You'll be used to working behind the bar, then-, won't you?" I swallowed my mouthful of egg and bacon before replying.

'He perhaps, didn't mean it like that,' I continued.

'Huh! I don't know about that. Anyway. I came to pay my respects to Alfie. He was an elder brother but he looked out for me when our step parents left for Australia.'

'They walked out then?'

'No, but I'd finished at Uni and they must have felt

their days as parents were over for them. I didn't want to go to Aus. I could've but it was Alfie who let me stay at his flat until I got a position with Children in Need. I went to Africa shortly after he started work on the beach. I was so pleased for him. He wrote and said he was really enjoying himself and that they'd kept him for another season.' I listened to Maria as I ate my breakfast and considered her life already to have been more exciting than mine to date.

I'd been out with Meila twice and was already tied to that mast of exclusive love for her. I envied dan, only later, who metaphorically found plenty of pebbles on the beach-the girlfriend variety, but was able to move on. I never considered until alter that it was Maria who showed concern for my well-being. Maria now the one waiting for me after the shock of the boat sinking. Though she was the one who nearly drowned.

'He was so organized,' she continued. He'd been cutting the grass in the churchyard and now he's buried there. Her eyes moistened, as she spoke, but she continued.

'I was going to return to Ireland, but then I met with the police and they gave me the few belongings that Alfie left, including a diary I don't think they looked at it thoroughly. I found a note in the cover, which Alfie must have written in rough. He wasn't a confident letter writer. I remember he prepared letters in rough several times before he actually committed them yo paper and envelope.

Four people sat on the table next to us. While we'd been talking a couple holding Coke cans stopped to watch the TV nearby. We were a bit in the public eye.

'I'd rather not talk about it here Phil, but you need to know that the Sea View isn't the sleepy holiday hotel it appears to be. Could we meet after at the Cliff Side one evening?'

'Yes, of course.'

'There'll be a quiet corner where no one can listen in. It's about something Alfie discovered and what he was going to tell me in his letter.'

'I have to wait Maria to see what the doctor says about returning to work. Would Thursday – that's tomorrow be okay?' I said as much as to reassure myself of the day it was now.

'Can we see tomorrow, about seven. Is that all right? I mean if they don't keep you in.' I was beginning to feel a bit more upbeat now.

'Yes, that's great Cliff side is within easy walking distance.'

'We'd perhaps best exchange numbers,' Maris picked up her mobile from the table. I retrieved mine from a buttoned pocket in the khaki trousers.

'Mine's 0776943351,' she said. I typed it in and called

her back so she could store my number.

A most "popular read," category for the novel *"Dancing on the Beach,"* By Sam Grant," from promotekdbook.com. A kindle/e-book site in North America. Membership of 60,000, in 2018.

STATION ENCOUNTER

It was a hurried exit from the flat. Burning the toast, setting off the smoke alarm and flying out of the front door. A lateness detective looking for evidence would have noted the hasty tying of shoes on the wall by the front gate, mouth still chewing on the remains of buttered toast. Verbal expletives expressed dropping the car keys on the pavement. A jamming of the car seat belt, causing further delay. Clues aplenty about driven by lateness. Planning the future. Visualizing imagining a parking space before you set out. As you arrive a car pulls out, or a space appears spectacularly in a row of cars. Reserved, prepared for you by some cosmic helper. There were occasions when this worked for me. Not today. It was too late to prepare for what was now the present, as I drove into the packed station car park. It meant an excursion to the very end of the park. And a squeeze into a space by the railings other drivers avoided.

The station clock's minute hand on the platform caught my eye as it jumped to eight twenty-six. This reduced anxiety. My train was due at eight thirty-five. I went to the waiting room. A recent box shaped addition. Inside rows of tables with bench seats. On the far wall a poster of a train hurtling through lush countryside with the bold claim.

"You can escape the crowd-Relax you're on track," running across the top. I sat in the corner next to a window with my back to the poster. The table height ideal for leaning on to scroll my Tablet. I intended to access the Head Office website, but became distracted by a cut-price holiday advert. It was a recent discovery of mine, that broadband was available in this corner of the Waiting Room.

The door clicked. I looked up. A young woman, I guess in her early twenties entered, in a blue leather coat and shoulder bag. Hair sort of encased in a woollen hat. Without looking around she came across, and oddly asked.

"Is this seat taken?" As if we were already in a train compartment. Not really seeing then why in an empty waiting room anyone should want to sit opposite me. I rationed my answer to-

'No.' I considered it wise to pretend to be absorbed in the advert, although I glanced across as she sat down. She placed the fingers of her hands momentarily together, but then lowered them before placing her elbows on the table with hands held to cheeks. I noticed there were no rings on her fingers. Deep blue eyes transmitted a pleading look.

'That's a neat looking tablet,' she said. 'I'm disturbing you. I expect you want to be alone,' she leant back with finger nails on the table's edge, but leant forward again, with a smile. Her eyes registered that overt interest level, which men can be reeled in on. The woollen type of beret she deftly removed, and dropped on the table. Blond hair tumbled down, to shoulder length. A shake of the head made it fall into place.

'Would you mind accessing a site for me?' she asked. 'The batteries flat on my I pad. Could you enter this? Don't worry I have a code.'

'Yes, that's not a problem,' I said. My curiosity as to why a code was required over ruled by that compliance technique women can use, when a sap, like me, finds the attractive. The strap curled away from her shoulder as she picked up her handbag. Its clasp clattered on the table. From a pocket, she produced a laminated card with large type showing a string of numbers and letters. Longer than my mobile phone number. After facing it towards me, her pink nail varnish visible, as she held the card for me to read. I was already in my mind questioning my helpfulness

—"Where was this going?" - But as if she read my thoughts she reassured me by saying,

'It's only a family message.'

"Lower case?" I heard myself ask, while her friendliness and perfume abducted rational male decision making.

'That's okay, you're very kind,' she said. I didn't

expect to see a video screen. A script appeared. A man's clear voice began, but then stopped to synchronize with the appearance of the text. The timbre not unlike that of the woman's, but more authoritative, announcing.

"You are now entering Real Time and exiting Earth planetary zone time."

A momentary pause. The pulsating glow from the moving script, brightened as if in receipt of a more powerful energy source. I'd never seen such luminosity on my I pad before **"The script will now run independently,"** the voice said. I looked for a person in the room, because the voice was no longer coming from my Tablet. It seemed to be near to where I was. The woman moved her arm along the bench behind and turned towards me.

'We already know you, everything will be all right,' she said. This statement kindled in me the memory of a captor who reassured a prisoner, when in an interview room, who had no chance of escape. I was unconvinced about everything being "all right." Although the Waiting Room appearance looked unchanged, it felt like its existence was moving away. I could not move my legs.

That dream sensation where you cannot run away had taken hold. Although I could see and move my hands. I took a deep breath and held it before letting it out. The woman said.

'Do not worry we are not here to harm you,' which

creepily worried me more, because although I couldn't see any person, I felt a powerful force holding me to the bench seat. I looked at the screen and there were moving pictures, which showed a life biography alongside the script—mine. That voice restarted, but with details about the solar system. Details about specific sectors, quadrants and the positioning of Venus and Mars relative to the Earth. This alien woman's face became animated whilst listening to the data, although meaningless to me. Frightening, because the script described my motivations on a review basis. Acceptable when good. Other times it depicted me as arrogant and oblivious to those around. Not a flattering ghost written biography, but the truth! That's really scary, who wants the world to know the unedited truth about your life? I was now already considering who else could gain access to this. Total strangers with access to my life detail. Yet I didn't feel that this woman/alien was a representative from St Peter or the other place.

There followed laughter.

'I find you amusing. You are right I am not a being from either of those places.'

'Incredible,' I replied. Now trying to hold back outright panic.

'I have some explaining to do. My name it has been decided is Adriana.' What did that mean, my name it has been decided, by what or whom? Not a name I was likely to forget in a hurry. She continued,

'Where do you think you are?' This seemed like a really dumb sort of question.

'I'm sitting in Stroud Waiting room, waiting for my train, of course,' I said. A leather belt around her coat slipped away as she stepped away from the table and raised arms opened the coat, which revealed a pink mini dress and tanned legs. Fake was my immediate thought. The arms once horizontal, opened the coat further, like a curtain, giving appreciation of feminine form. This distraction most likely intended to ensure my interest and attention. She turned more directly toward me, smiled- hands with fingers spread, palms rotated to face down. I felt that the room, and essence of my being there, now was subjected to a powerful control. Her arms as they lowered cancelled the light from the windows, left only artificial light from three ceiling lights.

'Now,' she said as she sat down opposite me once more. 'We are no longer in Stroud, we have entered "REAL TIME." - We have informed you of this, you were listening were you not?'

'Yes, but, where are we?' and in a pathetic little voice. 'How am I going to catch my train?' She ignored that question.

'Real Time, is the ability we have to make your time elastic. We can retrieve past events and we can extract from a time frame for purposes of research. We are able to convert molecules into constructs of our design and determination. Hence, we have kept for you the same environment,' she said, in speech fashion. 'Thanks, 'I said, as if being handed an unwanted drink, but thinking it wise to go along with the situation. Beginning now feeling like some organism, but with consciousness, in the petri dish of a scientist. 'It is because you are ordinary, a plausible individual James. You don't mind me calling you by your first name, do you?

'No, but I'm not so keen on the ordinary, plausible description.' She seemed amused and smiled, before asking,

'Do you find me attractive James? '

'My feeling is that you know that, 'I replied. You reliably access what I'm thinking,' I said.

'I expect you understand matters associated with attraction like heightened pulse.' I said attempting to elevate my ordinary status.

'We can intercept your neural pathways and intercept thought activity, before you are aware of receiving it. That is true. That feeling of attraction in the human race we have difficulty understanding. You were younger when we contacted you on previous occasions. You seemed, James, disinterested in your opposite specie, the female.'

'That's not true when did you contact me? More that

my life path meant I never met many of the opposite specie, as you put it.'

'I must return to our purpose,' she said. The man's voice, repeated, **"Return to purpose."**

'which made me re-consider who or what else was listening to this conversation.

'We need to enlist others to assist in breaking the news of our presence to the human species This is part of the evolutionary progression of humanity,' which made me feel like some abstract commodity, but I kept quiet. Your quest to explore other planets cannot be achieved without our assistance. We can transport people to the Moon, but also make life habitable on Mars. You-- James have been selected to promote this information. Representatives around your world are being selected to do this work. It will save many now on Earth and secure a safer future for your species. 'But I may not want to be your Noah,' I said.

'You remember this event, then,' she said.

'Not exactly. It's just embedded in our religious culture. Hey I've only been here twenty-five years.'

'We could take you back to the beginning of your human race.'

'No thanks, I'll pass on that,' I added hastily.

'There is more explaining to do. Now that we have made contact, we need to allow this knowledge to develop within you, before we proceed. We believe you, James will soon want to be part of this progression, when we reveal the risks to future Earth generations. We do not expect you to fully understand yet. I will allow you to catch your train. We believe you will want to know more. We will revisit.'

'What here, how?' I asked. This Adriana, creature, laughed.

'You are not anywhere, you are outside time and place.' Now twirling blond locks together and burying them back into that woollen hat. It occurred to me that it was something like a military beret. I was not convinced as they say that she came in peace. There was no mention of a star command fleet, yet this did cross my mind, which she picked up on.

'No in time, you will understand we come in peace,' she said. Those were her last words, before her arms and hands faced upwards moved in a reverse procedure, now making the window light reappear. Evidently with her/its mission accomplished, that was it. I'd wanted to ask more questions, I realized. The guile, the capturing of a man's attention, enticement. persuasion all made me believe Adriana was an actual woman, but how could this be? Footsteps could be heard coming down the metal stairway outside. Adriana turned smiled and waved at me, whilst leaving via the waiting room door. The tablet showed the picture clock at eight thirty.

"The train now arriving at platform one is the eighty thirty-six for Swindon," came from the platform loudspeaker. I switched my pad off placing it in my inside pocket before standing up and walking towards the door.

First appeared in short story form, in 2015. Later became a Chapter in Galactic Mission, 2017 and begins James Walters encounter with Adriana – "The Empress of Earth and all planets circling the solar system."

Author notes.

This story appears as a chapter in Galactic Mission by Sam Grant. A short story entry before publication of the complete science fiction novel in 2017.

SECRET CAVE

Halyards beat against the flag poles set out along the harbour wall. Shrouds caught by the wind made that tuneless chord that spelt of unsettled weather. The pram dinghy nearly got taken out of my hands when upturned. Rainwater previously captured exited - in a rush.

Tony was late, but since his dating Katrina unreliability was expected. They were in love, as if that excused recognition of others, who were not so engaged or trapped. I could see that this state might be seen as reasonable for winter months with Sea Spray stilted on dry land with no place to go. Existence no longer driven by that most important activity on the planet. Namely racing or sailing Silver Spray, whenever time allowed.

'Katrina would like to get to know you Steve.' Tony said, earlier, to break me in. The truth be known that one person could not manage the boat without some extra muscle. But I'd felt that his friendship with Katrina should be kept distant from our boat share. It was a four-way share ownership. Tony, Peter, Karl and me. Outside of race times each was allowed a Sunday to take the boat out. You did need a crew member to let go of the mooring and handle the sails. On race days three people were required. We took it on a rota basis with each of us dropping out alternatively, in the four weeks to keep the on-board weight down. Peter invariably helmed, simply because he was brilliant at it. Tony was joining me today to go to Blackberry cove. It was primarily to revisit a cave, which we found by chance on a previous weekend visit. We planned to leave after I finished work at midday.

'Oh, and by the way Katrina's joining us Steve.' I was in a meeting with a group of

managers when I intercepted my smart phones jingle.

'Is that a business call Steven?' My first name was called out by the area manager, in an attempt to grasp bogus friendship from a business associated relationship.

'No- Doug, caught me unawares- forgot to switch it off, that's all,' I replied, but promptly texted OK before cutting the phone----but was that it? No, it wasn't. Claire pointed a recriminatory finger, out of sight of Doug. Why did these meetings have to be so? juvenile. Just then, on the slipway, my phone vibrated my pocket. Furniture

of earlier daily event was still in my mind, when I recognized Tony's number.

'Turn around Steve - **"You've been framed."** They were three stories up on the multi-storey, that's Katrina and Tony. He in cutaway jeans and tee shirt, phone in hand, and leant over the rail. Katrina dressed in knotted blouse and wrap around mini-skirt. A dress statement, however, that looked more suitable for going to a pub than to clamber about on a boat.

She smiled and waved with her right trainer placed on the lower rail and one hand round Steve. At least she wasn't wearing footwear that might damage the deck! Tony with cupped hands shouted down.

'Bit late-- do you think it's OK to go out to the beach?'

'We can motor if it's too squally,' I called back. Their faces disappeared, while they walked down the stairs to ground level.

'Don't look at me like that Tony, I'm wearing shorts and bikini underneath,' she said when they appeared together on the slipway. Tony, who was dangerously smitten made conciliatory noises.

'That's fine Katra. I just said that you'd best wear trainers not shoes.'

'Nothing else needed? Are we skinny dipping? - Hi Steve,' she called out, waving in my direction.

'Hi Katrina, glad you could make it.

I never "ever" understood what Tony saw in Katrina- as a serious girl-friend. She was a picture to look at, yes. Model figure, which could have stepped out of a fashion swim wear shoot. Long curled eyelashes, chestnut hair, slim legs. You just knew that those rose bud lips could pout enticingly at any camera.

Problem was that she had stepped out of the calendar. Beauty and desirability were attached to what was, a difficult and demanding personality. I'd never tell

Tony that. Probably get a smack in the face if I did, or the sharp end of his tongue. It was best to go with the flow, so to speak.

'The waters really cold further out,' I said. 'I doubt whether you'll want to swim.'

'Not even a little skinny dip?' Katrina replied with that look of a child denied a treat.

I unlocked the security chain and cleared it from the oars. Tony released first one galvanized rowlock, then reached across to the other While his right hand rested on the middle thwart he flipped the far one up into position. I slid the blades forward and laid the oar handles well down into the boat. There was a wheel set into the keel, which made for an easy run down the slipway.

Tony and me picked up the bow and walked it down, before we released it a few feet from the water. It splashed noisily outwards, but I held the painter to pull it back to the slipway. 'You'd better sit in the stern Kat,' said Tony.

'What about my shoulder bag?' she asked.

'Give it here, Katrina,' I said. She pulled the strap over her head and handed it to me and to place under the middle thwart. Tony, held her hand as he boarded. 'Are there life jackets. I would feel safer wearing a life jacket?'

'There're on the boat, Kat,' replied Tony. 'You can put one on once we're aboard. It's not far to row. That's it there.' Tony pointed to our small yacht. A clinker-built boat painted in cream with weathered varnished coach roof and cockpit. Only about two hundred metres from the shore. Tony assisted Katrina aboard. I followed and Tony pushed us away from the slipway. Once alongside Tony was first to board Silver Spray.

'You did say it's got an engine?' asked Katrina as she held my shoulder and then grabbed Tony's hand to get aboard

'Yep, but there's plenty of wind.'

'Tony, said, that I could steer once we get out of the harbour.'

'I said, "only" that I expected you could,' replied Tony. Katrina turned back towards me.

'You'll show me Steve, won't you? Tony's mean. He told me off for looking into shop windows when I was driving his car through town- I've never been in an accident, but he has.' Tony kept silent.

We were together, standing in the cockpit, putting on life jackets when she asked insistently 'Why is it called a secret cave?'

'Because we don't believe anyone else has discovered it before. There was something in the second cave, but the tide was on the rise'

'And the torch battery fading,' I said. '|I don't know Tony, that there was anything there, other than cave walls. You imagined that you saw something. It was just shadows that jumped behind the torchlight.'

'Katra, Katra, a girl's voice came across the water from the slipway.

'Prezzie,' Katrina called back and waved frantically.

'It's Priscilla.' A girl, in her late teens, about the same age as Katrina, who I'd chronicled as the more sensible, was now standing on the slipway waving.

'Can I come? Can I come with you?'

'No,' said Tony. Loud enough for her to hear. I called back.

'We won't be back 'til this evening.'

'I don't mind-! Katra, I've got the video on my phone from that gig at the Pirate and Fiddle.'

'You've got to let her join us, Tony then!' said Katrina, whilst she grabbed his arm.

'I'm not fetching her.' The shock of Tony not doing as Katrina asked perhaps caught me off balance. I received a plaintiff, winsome smile. Like some prey mesmerised by a cobra I found myself uncoiling the painter from around its cleat. Pulled the pram alongside and jumped in the centre to avoid overturning it. There was less fuss from Priscilla when she boarded, than with Katrina, after the metal keel runner grated on to the slip. Once aboard Priscilla disappeared into the cabin with "Katra." Excited cries and giggles came out as they watched the video together.

'It's better Tony,' I said that it's not just Katrina with us.

'Why?'

'It just is.'

'And the secret cave isn't secret anymore?'

'Look Tony you brought Katrina with you. I never asked you to. They'll perhaps stay on board when we get there, anyway. That's what I'm hoping.'

Tony slipped the mooring after he raised the jib sail. A breeze across the harbour was brisk enough to reach a little way along while Tony winched the mainsail up. I went about as we approached the harbour wall and we had a direct run across to the harbour mouth.

'Hey, what's happening?' A cry came from the cabin. We bounced in the harbour mouth after a launch sped in before it throttled down. Its bow wave disturbed the calm.

'You'd be better up here. You could get sea sick down there,' said Tony.

That was the last thing we wanted-sick all over the cabin. There was an easterly swell, which has been known to induce sea sickness.

'Katrina came out of the cabin first. They'd both taken their tee shirts off, which revealed bikini tops. Both in white shorts.

'Can we sit up on the deck, asked Katrina?'

'No replied Tony, you'll fall overboard.' Katrina

smirked disapproval. We'd brought the pram dinghy which because of following swell kept pushing forward. Nearly hitting the transom before it slipped back. Each time this made the painter tug aggressively with the forward thrust of the yacht. A heavy swell to start with, but it was a running reach all the way across to Blackberry Cove and this meant that direct approach could be made. Threat of storm weather didn't materialize. Priscilla said to Katrina,

'He's bossy.'

'No, he's just annoyed because you're here,' was Katrina's answer.

'Are you annoyed with me Tony?' Priscilla was stood in the hatchway between cabin and deck. Katrina though engrossed with texting on her smart phone, whilst sat on the opposite bench to me.

'No! did Katrina say that?' Tony held the tiller held behind him, in an attempt to cope with the inevitable yawing caused by the swell. Priscilla didn't reply, but just nodded back to Katrina, who returned to her main activity of texting. I felt justified in not having a female crew member aboard when racing, after dealings with Katrina. How could you be aboard a yacht and spend all your time texting? There was so much going on, like the taut snap and vibration across the mainsail as we caught successive blasts of wind. That forward flow of the yacht through the sea and panoramic view of coastline in the bay. How could Katrina find time to text? I didn't feel that I held a misogynistic view, about this! All buffeting stopped as we went under the lee of the land.

'Thank goodness for that,' said Katrina, who'd finished a text and decided to share more interest in what was going on around.

'Look,' called out Priscilla, the beach's empty.' A short stretch of beach could be seen beyond the white wave break.

'You can only reach it by sea,' said Tony. 'Those cliffs are sheer.'

'It's like a private beach, then. That's cool.' I chipped in with,

'there's a rising tide which could cool the water.' Katrina trailed a hand in the water.

'That's cold. I'm not swimming in that,' she said.

'You don't have to,' said Tony. We'll go to the beach in the dinghy. I expect water will have warmed from the sun on the beach through the day.' My hope that they'd stay aboard quashed by this suggestion.

'All four of us?' asked Priscilla. 'What about the yacht?' She was more clued up than I'd thought.

'There's a spare anchor rope in the fo'c'sl'e, we're near enough to tie it to Sea Spray and run it ashore,' I said to Tony more than anyone else. The risk was that currents and the wind on the yacht might each cause the anchor to drag. A line ashore was a safety precaution.

We went ashore with me rowing, Priscilla in the bow. Katrina and Tony fed out the line. It was quite heavy going because there was a cross wind. The bow crunched into the beach and Priscilla jumped out and with a cry of –

'It's freezing here,' followed by sharp intakes of breath. Katrina stayed aboard until we'd lifted the dinghy on to the beach.

'Your ladyship can disembark now,' said Priscilla. It was a sentiment that I might have shared, but felt better left unspoken. Out of hearing of the others

Tony said,

'Are we still going to show them the cave and the early grotto part.

'I don't see that we've a choice. We said we're sailing over and that was the bait you used to get Katrina to join us. Anyway, Tony we mightn't be able to go if they don't want to dive into the pool. I wouldn't mind if this was the case. There was a grotto type area with small stalactites and stalagmites in the cave at beach level. That might satisfy Katrina's curiosity

'We could just say that it's a secret cave that reveals itself when the tide goes out,' I continued.

'Would you prefer to do that?'

'No, I want to have another look. We had to go almost

the moment we arrived last time, because of the tide.' We were interrupted by Katrina,

'Where's the secret then?'

'You mean what's the secret?' don't you said Priscilla.

'There's no one about. We could go skinny dipping,' said Katrina, once more.

'I'm not doing that. Stripping in front of them. How could you Katrina?

'I like the sense of freedom. We'd be all the same.' Priscilla wasn't convinced

'It might give them ideas that, you know, we're-'

'Available? Tony knows when I'm not. Don't you?' Katrina raised her voice to get his ear. But also, no doubt because she wanted to get us to hear what was being said to Tony.

'Know what?'

'Know that I'm not that easy about getting my kit off.' Tony reddened. He was not really smart enough to stand up to Katrina, when she goaded him. It was also made clear who called the shots in their sex life-Katrina. I decided to shift the talk back to the secret cave

'Look, we made a discovery some weeks back. Over there.' I pointed to a dark opening in the rocks at the cliff base. That's covered once the tides in. It's known locally as the smugglers cave.

'It'll be dark and creepy inside,' said Priscilla.

'I've brought two waterproof torches. We left the far pool last time, because the torch battery gave out and the tide was coming in fast. The cliff, beneath the first cave pool went down about four metres and then there was a gap, at the bottom between the two sides. When I surfaced, on discovering this Tony said,

'If, the waters not that deep this side it probably won't be on the other side.' It didn't follow this supposed logic. Nor did it stop me getting under the ledge and surfacing in a much larger cave on the other side. The water depth there was at least seven metres. It was reckless by any definition. I couldn't hold my breath much above a minute under water.

'It's not deep but you have to dive down and swim under the ledge at the bottom, I said.

'Really?' said Katrina- 'And there's- like a grotto on the other side? Now that sounds exciting. It's like all right to breathe once you get there?'

'Oh, yes, said Tony. You can feel like a breeze from above. I was expecting a less enthusiastic response from Priscilla, but Katrina, said,

'You won't have any trouble will you Pressie? You were in the water sports team at college.'

'Is it cold and smelly?' she asked.

'It smells a bit of seaweed, and there's water running down the walls, but it's a cave and you can stand up and walk about inside,' said Tony. The clincher was perhaps a sudden squall of wind and rain that swept on to the beach and made us run toward the cave. The darkness needed some adjusting to, even with the torch light. which danced across the ridged red cave wall when we entered.

'Look, there're small stalactites growing at the back,' called out Priscilla.'

'They're stalagmites,' said Tony. 'How can you tell the difference anyhow?' asked Priscilla. I was glad that it was Tony who explained a way of remembering the difference.

'It's quite easy if you remember that stalactites come down. As in women's-

'Yes, you needn't explain Tony,' said Katrina. 'I don't wear them in the summer, so that won't be happening! She turned to Priscilla with despairing disdain.

'Does it end there?' Asked Katrina. She followed Tony's torch light across the inside.

'That's what we thought,' said Tony. He walked towards a large boulder which appeared to obstruct any possibility of a path. It was Tony, this time who backed on to the boulder and raised his arms to extend across the boulder as I had on our previous visit. There was no reason originally to do this other than to see if I could reach the sides of the boulder with both arms extended. I couldn't, but this action caused the boulder to pivot to the right and create an opening. That same affect occurred for Tony. A gap was wide enough for him to manoeuvre sideways into the next cave where he shone the torch back.

'That's a fantastic discovery,' said Priscilla.

'Will it stay open? That's what worries me,' asked Katrina. 'Once we're inside can we get out?'

'It won't close,' I said until the tide enters from the beach.

'And how long will that be?'

'Two hours at least,' I said, with the tide further down the beach. We've got longer.' This appeared to satisfy Katrina but Priscilla said,

'That seems okay. Except there's no signal. Priscila held her smart phone in one hand.

'No problem, my watch's waterproof, I said. We can check on the time.' They looked one to the other. Curiosity got the better of Katrina.

'We can have a look, Prezzie.'

They followed after Tony. Light from our torches displayed the main pool, which stretched across from a slate platform. A smaller pool lay immediately ahead.

'It's quite warm,' said Katrina who'd removed a flip flop to test the water in the first pool.

'Yes,' I said that's what encouraged me to dive in after swimming across.'

'There was a panic when we reached the other side

because the torch started to fade.

'We never investigated any further,' said Tony.

'You said there were shadows. Didn't you?' Questioned Katrina.

'Shadows from the torch - until it faded,' I said. That seemed a reasonable assumption.

'These two torches have brand new batteries.' A sweep of my torch showed the outer limits of the cave. About twenty metres going back to a seaweed and barnacle encrusted rock face, but with no more than eight metres wide, at the entrance. Constant tidal impact had layered the sides and hollowed out the back of the cave to more like ten metres. Sand was heaped there, and at the back the cave's floor further was smattered with rock pools.

'Shine the torch in front of us Tony, not on the back wall,' said Katrina. There was that green slimy weed on the rocks which led toward the main pool.

'It's slippy,' she called out. 'Oh my God!'

'If we walk forward four across and hold hands we should manage,' I said.

'We'll be alright if we hold each other's hands,' said Katrina, to Priscilla.

'You two just need to shine your torches on the path ahead!

'Do we need a piece of string in case we get lost?' asked Priscilla.

'Perhaps the Minotaur's waiting?' continued Katrina.

Their laughter echoed back and forth around the cave. It was, our intention that the two of us would return. I admit to disappointment after Tony called to say that he was bringing Katrina. I'd sort of hoped that it would just be the two of us. A secret that would remain with us. There were prehistoric caves in the area. Perhaps if there were more stalactites and stalagmites and a few rock indentations. Perhaps, even teeth of prehistoric animals, like that of the sabre-toothed tiger or mammoth we could start a tourist attraction. I admit to the further development of this idea into a ferry charge to take visitors to the beach. A budding Disney theme park muse halted by a scream from Katrina. A rock crab disturbed by our presence fell to the cave's floor with a clatter and scrambled away

'It won't bite you,' said Tony. 'It's too small.'

'Look,' I said. Torch batteries don't have a long life. I'd like to dive down to the other side. I'll put the torch in the water and then you three will see it when you dive under the ledge.' After the shriek from the crab incident there was some doubt that Katrina would be prepared to dive into the water, but Priscilla was the courageous one.

'Katra, I'll dive down with Tony's torch and wait for you.'

'That's a great idea.' Before Tony could contribute

either way Katrina grabbed the torch and handed it to Priscilla.

'Go on then Steve,' she said. I placed the torch on the cave floor and removed my tee shirt, as did Tony. The two girls their shorts.

'Okay,' I said. Count to five before you dive. Tony you can follow Katrina and Priscilla.'

I made a smooth entrance into the pool, which was just below the surrounding rock ledge. I felt the rock wall with my left hand on the way down until my hand touched the cave floor. I held the torch upwards whilst I clung to the other side, but only momentarily. I let go and within seconds surfaced on the other side. A thrust back and forth in the water enabled me to scramble up into the new cave. Complete darkness surrounded me as I leant forward and dipped the torch into the water, but almost immediately Katrina spluttered to the surface ahead of Priscilla; followed by Tony, whose torch helped lighten the cave. My torch I placed to one side to assist them out of the water and on to the new cave's ledge.

'It's quite warm in here, but it stinks of fish and seaweed,' said Katrina. Both the girl's appearances had changed. Long hair now flattened into a cap-like flatness by the water. They'd both managed to bring hair ties and after a shaking of heads wrapped these like pipe cleaners around the bedraggled tails of hair.

It was Tony's torch that caught the fish bones scattered on ledges around the cave. Large fish. I imagined that they might be the bones of pollock, cod or perhaps even sea bass.

'Look at all those fish bones,' said Katrina. 'Do you think they died in here? Like got trapped.' I was standing near to a ledge which held about ten fish bone shapes.

'They might have swum in on the tide and got caught, but there's no flesh remaining and they don't look that old,' I said

'That means that something or someone's eaten them,' said Tony.

'Do you really think so? What?' We were not left in the dark for long. There was a shriek like that of a trapped animal that came from a tunnel on the far side.

'What the hell's that,' said Tony. A shriek which ended with a shrill high note, but this seemed impossible. In fact, the idea that the cave was inhabited I'd never thought about. I shivered, involuntarily. Maybe the others experienced a shiver from fear spontaneously like me, activated by some primal response, which we retain. Tony's torch light caught Katrina's wide-eyed look

'Those bare fish bones. Are they the remains of a meal?'

'It's impossible, said Tony. In contradiction to his first response. 'There can't be creatures here. I mean creatures that are not known about.' It was a trumpeted shriek like that of a panicked elephant.

I realized afterwards that the shriek and shrill note was a call. We'd been detected by whatever was living in the tunnels set into the cliff face. The most obvious conclusion was that the bones, scattered across the cave were the remains of a meal or meals. These creature's dependant on the rise and fall of the tide to fish in much the way humans had for thousands of years. Next to one stash of bones were the storks of seaweed. A diet quite capable of sustaining an animal adapted to such a diet. This jigsaw was completed later on reflection, but not at that time. I shined my torch across to the side behind the pool. There were three tunnels and the shriek could have come from any one.

'Whatever, it is, it's not some trapped sea bird. Not with a powerful screech like that,' said Katrina.

'I'm scared, but curious, if that makes sense,' I said.

'You're allowed to be scared, but don't get too curious, Steve,' said Tony. The pool separates us, but if whatever it is can swim across---'

We didn't have long to wait. A shadow came out of the furthermost cave and was almost invisible, until Tony shone the torch directly at it. A staccato shriek, heightened when the light met green eyes, that were set into a crocodile-like head. Small hands rather than paws at its sides, like a tyrannosaurus, but no more than three metres high. Orange scales, with a black under belly, for it stood supported by sturdy hind legs. A scraped noise was made by its long tail that swept sufficiently to be visible on each side of the main body. It related to that experience with cats when tail movement is related to anger before a fight and the creature was moving toward the main pool. Stopped and gave another piercing shriek, when the light from my torch reached its eyes as well as from Tony's torch.

'It doesn't know light. It's confined to the dark. We're scaring it said Tony.'

There came a sound more rumble than shriek from further in the tunnel.

'That could be daddy croc,' said Katrina. 'I want to get out of here! They might feed on fish, but want a change of diet.'

'What if they follow us into the water?' whispered Priscilla. The beast, remained transfixed, by the torch light, whilst emitting intermittent almost plaintive shrieks.

'Look. It's no more than 5 metres down to the ledge. They won't be able to get under. You three make a dive for it. I'll keep my torch trained on its eyes. The idea sounded heroic, but now seems terrifying when I look back. Sometimes quick decisions are the best.

'Don't stay a second longer than us,' said Priscilla,

who was the only one who appeared to share concern.

'Go, then,' I said. They three dived in, whilst I noticed that the beast had now turned to meet its larger version, which was both taller and broader. Although some way from the pool. This, adult version, I presumed, went down on all fours and was making for the pool at speed. It was in attack mode and I dived into the pool. The others had by now scrambled under the ledge, but when I reached the upper opening I shone the torch and the scales of the monster shone like phosphorus as it rapidly approached. I felt a rush of water as its snout snapped shut, missing my leg by millimetres. When I surfaced gasping and gulping in the adjacent cave, I felt a hand grip my arm and then take hold of my hand. I looked up to see the look of relief on Priscilla's face.

'Where are Katrina and Tony?' I gasped.

'They're outside.'

'They didn't hang about.' She helped me to my feet. A concerned look, before she embraced me. Both of us like creatures from the sea dripping with water.

'That was very brave Steve,' she said, before she kissed my neck.

'Aren't you worried that these creatures might come after us.' I asked.

'I don't think they can get under that narrow gap. Do you Steve?' She smiled and held my arm momentarily, before drawing back. It was probably at this point when Silver Spray, as the priority for the summer probably fought for poll position. It seemed natural to hold hands as we walked out toward the bright light of the beach.

'They're like Plato's cave dwellers. They don't know light. Not even shadows. That is their world in there. Safe from the modern world. I think we should keep the cave a secret,' said Priscilla.

'What about Katrina and Tony?'

'If they mention what happened to anyone we can say that it's a made-up joke. No one will believe what's in that cave. How could anyone possibly believe what we've just experienced? We'll say that it's a joke made up by Tony and Katrina. it's likely then to remain a secret Don't you think Steve?' I realized Priscilla was probably right. A prolonged kiss, before we went out to be with Katrina and Tony,' was confirmation that this would be our plan.

WITCH TAKES OVER VILLAGE

Even back then, the village, merged with the main town. Houses sprawled from the harbour, along a main road until it met the village. A street with a pub, on the right followed by a row of shops. On the other side a wall with arrow headed railings. These segregated school from road. Finally, situated along a private road terraced houses took over where the school playground came to an end.

There were three key shops. Radshaws, a grocer, which sold liquorice in string form, tubes, pipes and reels. Four black jack chews for a penny, banana splits, two a penny, assorted sherbet product. Animal shaped chocolate bars and raspberry powdered drink in a sachet to mix with water. A resident aunt, said this would rot my insides and teeth. She was probably right. A vital second shop was Cooper's, the Post Office. Graduation to real reading other than comic strip was a kind of forced event. This accidentally occurred with a purchase of the Wizard, which instead of bubbled comic strip was filled with stories and serial chapters. A struggle to read, at first. Stories could be about alien forces who had conquered the world. A fight back would be in progress with an armed Flying Scotsman, concealed in a tunnel. The train would steam out to fire at this alien force. Also, a story about an individual commando behind enemy lines, who bombed installations with the mortar launcher hidden in a split log. A phoenix like champion football player, who scored crucial goals in the second half. Today, such astonishing performance subject to a test for possible use of illegal substances.

One head teacher did complain about hand writing—"It's indecipherable." Not that this prevented a hankering for a Parker duo-fold Pen in black. Savings driven by the desire to save up and to buy this exquisite pen, then on display at WH Smith's. A third key premises was the village toy shop. This was run by a silver haired lady, whose vital roll in retail was the supply of toy pistol caps. Western movies and comics inspired enactment of fight scenarios. Pirate ship pistols, which doubled as highwayman guns, also needed caps. Hammer action enabled several caps to be loaded at a time, which meant better smoke and fire effect. These caps purchased by myself and a friend, who lived in the village. It was dubbed the frontier store, because it was the last one in the village adjacent to a meandering road which led to the beach. A descriptive narrative that has no immediate relevance to this story. A banal normality, alongside extraordinary, dimensional and apparitional phenomena. This a peaceable snapshot two years onward from black nightmare. Then I was sleeping alone in an extraordinarily large bedroom, away from sisters. It was probably accepted that a boy was a strange, peculiar being amongst three sisters and formidable aunts. An aunt, the one in question, was lodged with the family in another largish bedroom. Possibly between either flats or relationships, but the television was on ITV. There was the novelty of adverts and aunt viewed programmes with popular appeal. BBC news and The Brains Trust, were not must view programmes for my aunt. She also kept a good supply of Fox's glacier mints. Not usually a child's favourite but preferable to no sweets at all, after weekly pocket money ran out.

In other years foreign students occupied aunt's room. They, on occasion, were exchanged for one or other of my sisters, who went to a complementary family in Sweden, France or Germany. In particular, this was considered a good idea by me. That is the exchange of my sisters for French, German or Swedish girls. I fell in love, because most likely, they were pleasant toward me. Not so inclined to boss. Swedish Olga, used to sit on the settee with her legs curled beneath, and smile in my direction. A more petite version of Swedish girls that could throw British men into paroxysms of ecstasy with svelte figure, and naturally blonde Scandinavian hair when they first visited Britain. When outdoors and in the rain, she would wrap her coat, in a protective way, around me. I was, "most" definitely in love with Olga. She was seventeen to my seven years of age.

Francoise, a dark Gallic French girl stayed in a later year. I kind of admired her impudence towards adults. She bought a brown paper bag of plums from the village, instead of leaving the stones in the bag after eating them she lined them up around the edge of the bath. For this she received a telling off from mother. Francoise would invite me into her room—open the faded blue curtains; grab the window handles and lift up the sashed window, which overlooked the garden. Then produce a blue packet of Galoises cigarettes, light one of these pungent offerings but then offer me those miniature cocktail cigarettes with red, blue and yellow tips. The tobacco being much milder. Now, several summers on, I was again in love. Francoise, with her black curly hair, and olive skin, in contrast to the fair-haired Olga. She may have befriended me, after lost popularity with more senior members of the female hierarchy. That's mother, and sisters in situ.

French boys, on occasion, stayed for the summer. That their parents paid for food and board, and were older, enhanced I felt their status in the household, above mine. I remember, Pierre. He, was fifteen. A little older than my second eldest sister, who returned from a friend's party with a box of Black Magic. I was allowed the marzipan, which was the least liked, but Pierre, was left out of even the offer of a chocolate coated marzipan. Later that week, he produced a Cadbury Dairy Milk chocolate box, opened it, and smilingly offered my sister a chocolate. These chocolates moulded from earth in the garden to be realistically inserted in the paper wrapper holders of the empty box. I can't remember whether my sister attempted to eat one, but this action, put paid to any development of girl, boy friendship between her and Pierre.

Actual event is related to when I was about six. My bed was in the middle of this large bedroom opposite a squat black coke stove with double doors. A ridged metal top was useful to soften Plasticine in winter. It was possible, with doors open, to toast bread on a long brass fork, provided you sat well back. Outside this bedroom door there was—for the eyes of a child, a ball room sized landing. My parent's bedroom, was opposite with an on-suite bathroom and toilet. Another bedroom and then opposite to this, the door led to the aunt/student bedroom, pre-mentioned. Six stairs down there was a small landing, with a bedroom to the left. Opposite a toilet, set back along a very long corridor. An arch in the centre of this small landing displayed a full-length mirror. A space which led to a corridor with lengthy cupboard space. The servants could have hidden away from view, whilst putting away or fetching clothes, sheets, bedding and table linen. Except that there were no servants! My aunts remonstrated with mother, about this - 'How can you possibly run such a large house Dorothy. Cook for a family of six, and lodge foreign students, without a servant in sight?' they would say to their sister-in-law, my mother. The foreign students when not exchanged, paid to stay, with my two elder sisters assisting with the housework. Mother perhaps preferred not to have servants. Younger sister and myself were like a second family. Born to the end of the Second World War. Maybe, pre-war, father's family employed servants. The aunts, said emphatically--- they would not have run such a large house without servant in sight.

There, I was alone, in this vast bedroom with two long windows on the outer wall with a large bay window overlooking the garden at the far end. Small children can be scared of the dark. I wasn't particularly scared to start with. That was until there were recurring dreams about a witch. She entered my awareness while asleep and dreaming about walking through the village when it became dark. I would not have been allowed to be there in the evening, so this was odd. My mother on occasion was apt to leave me in shops, and return home without me. After realizing her absence would manage at four or five to walk back along the road travelled by the double decker bus. Through the winding street, past the shops, and up the hill to home. There was no recognition from my mother, that I was lost or missing. Today this condition would probably be diagnosed as post-natal depression, following on from the birth of my younger sister.

The dream or more explicitly nightmare occurred fairly consistently. Darkness would descend suddenly and coincide with the witch's appearance. I knew immediately that I needed to get away from the village and head for home. In this dream situation a strategy was developed on the walk back home to pretend to go up the middle road leading to the front door entrance and then to double back and follow the higher road, which led to the back entrance. The witch, I hoped would continue up the middle road to the front entrance. In the dream re-assurance was felt only when the lights from the back bedrooms of the house could be seen from the road. The back gate led into a kitchen garden. Safety would rapidly be displaced when my feeling was that the witch was in the garden.

On dry sunny day blankets and sheets were spread over Rosemary shrubs which followed a curved path to a kitchen and main garden. These, I considered, gave cover and might allow me to crawl on hands and knees up the path, hopefully out of sight of the witch. That she would be attracted to dance and sing incantations to her dark heart's content, around a toadstool circle on a nearby lawn. Through the back door and on to the concreted floor of the outer pantry. Then, a sense of relief would kick in. With those heavy legs of sleep, I would attempt to tiptoe into the relative safety of the kitchen. Next, to open the green beige door, which led to a corridor alongside a panelled main stairway. On the left-hand wall, a large, tapestry of Mary with the baby Jesus was reassuring. In darkness now but I knew she would gaze with adoration at the haloed baby. I also knew, in this very active dream that I should be in bed. This concept of the dream state, not realized whilst I ran up the main flight of stairs-- to turn on the small landing and race up the six stairs, which led to the main landing and the hoped-for safety of the bedroom.

The reality, was that I was already in bed, asleep. In my mind I could hear the witch on the landing. The door to the bedroom was never fully closed. My mother perhaps, a-tuned to my nocturnal disturbances, would leave it open for when I left the bedroom for the landing.

'Look, Look, there she is,' I would cry out, a dream, which continued when in a waking state. The open door, though could now give the witch easier access. It was several witch dreams down the road before I developed a witch dispersal technique. The door handle would appear to turn, signalling the witch's arrival. A troupe of players was imagined into existence. Musicians, dancers, jugglers and acrobats, who would attempt to get through the door, before the witch. Eye lids opened and shut.

This action was the signal to make them appear, I would glance furtively at the door. A juggler, who moved from side to side, to meet and catch twirled batons, was usually first to enter. Then, musicians, who shook ribbon tambourines. And strummed lutes, rather than guitars, I remember. Why should they not arrive in this bedroom it was large enough to accommodate them. My theory was that the witch would be outnumbered, on their arrival and be forced to return to the village. There were several encounters with the witch in my dreams, before I hit on imagining this arrival of players. Invited to enter my dream, when nightmare's intruded with sleep. The opening and shutting of eyes pressed insistence on this time and scene chang. A repeated action brought into focus the players arrival and receded a nightmare. Once they flowed into the room, they allowed me the choice of wakening fully to watch them, no longer petrified by the witch's presence or alternatively to fall asleep. They only appeared in the bedroom for the time I dreamt, as a child. Adults, are perhaps excluded from similar assistance.

{**Background note**} A story with dream content. Although written as fiction, experiences are taken from the author's life. Foreign students who stayed with the family was a constant. French, Swedish, German and Swiss nationality, mainly. One French boy who was sent by his mother returned on several occasions. The author's family was large and this French boy developed a friendship with a family who ran motor boats and beach rafts from Redgate Beach, Torquay. No longer accessible due to rock cliff falls across bridge access to beach.

Although not a great language speaker it never seemed unusual for the author to have a mixed nationality crew aboard ship. Perhaps living in a house with a flow of nationalities was preparation for this.

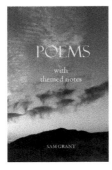

Lightning Source UK Ltd.
Milton Keynes UK
UKHW02f1506261018
331261UK00006B/140/P